THERE'S MOUNTING ANGER IN THE REGIONS ABOUT THE DEPLORABLE STATE OF OUR ROMAN ROADS!

L-LIES! I, LACTUS BIFIDUS, HAVE RESPONSIBILITY FOR ROMAN ROADS, AND I CANNOT ACCEPT THESE ALLEGATIONS!

SO I'D LIKE TO TAKE THIS OPPORTUNITY TO ANNOUNCE A SPECIAL ONE-OFF CHARIOT RACE!

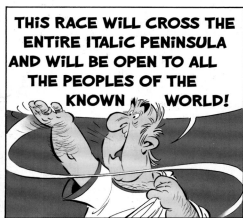

THIS RACE WILL CROSS THE ENTIRE ITALIC PENINSULA AND WILL BE OPEN TO ALL THE PEOPLES OF THE KNOWN WORLD!

IT WILL BE A SPLENDID SHOWCASE FOR THE EXCELLENT STATE OF OUR ROMAN ROADS!

THIS RACE IS A STROKE OF GENIUS! THERMOCUMULUS ALMOST HAD STEAM COMING OUT OF HIS EARS! DID IT COME TO YOU JUST LIKE THAT?

JUST LIKE THAT... I'M FULL OF IDEAS WHEN I FIRST WAKE UP!

THE ONLY PROBLEM IS WE NOW HAVE A RACE TO ORGANISE AND THE ROAD NETWORK'S A NIGHTMARE ...

I KNOW, I'M IN CHARGE OF IT.

THERE YOU ARE, LACTUS! I HOPE YOU HAVEN'T FORGOTTEN OUR ORGY WITH TIRAMISUS?

NO ORGY THIS EVENING, MOZZARELLA, I HAVE TO WORK!

REALLY? THAT'S NOT LIKE YOU!

WELL, AT LEAST IT MEANS I'LL SLEEP BETTER IN THE SENATE TOMORROW!

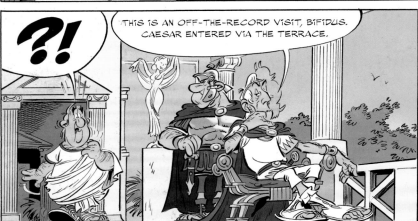

?!

THIS IS AN OFF-THE-RECORD VISIT, BIFIDUS. CAESAR ENTERED VIA THE TERRACE.

EXCELLENT IDEA OF YOURS, THIS RACE BETWEEN ROMANS, ITALICS AND BARBARIANS. AS A GREAT SPORTSMAN HIMSELF, CAESAR MIGHT EASILY HAVE THOUGHT OF IT.

UM... YES, I THOUGHT... WELL, CHARIOT RACES AT THE COLOSSEUM TEND TO GO ROUND IN CIRCLES ...

3A

OF COURSE, BIFIDUS, I NEEDN'T POINT OUT THAT VICTORY ABSOLUTELY MUST GO **TO A ROMAN!**

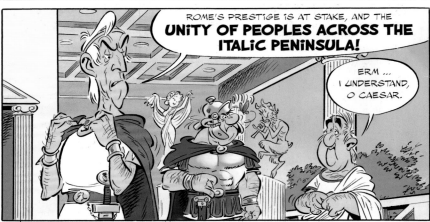

ROME'S PRESTIGE IS AT STAKE, AND THE **UNITY OF PEOPLES ACROSS THE ITALIC PENINSULA!**

ERM ... I UNDERSTAND, O CAESAR.

IF ROME IS DEFEATED, YOU'LL BE LEVELLING THE ROADS IN DISTANT CYRENAICA*. JUMP TO IT THEN, I WANT YOU ACTIVE, BIFIDUS!

* LIBYA

LACTUS, CAN YOU TELL ME WHAT'S GOING ON?

I'M GOING TO WAKE UP! I'M GOING TO WAKE UP! I'M GOING TO WAKE UP!

3B

CH   E

Colour by THIERRY MÉBARKI

Orion

ITALY ...

WHAT BETTER SYMBOL OF ITS DAZZLING CIVILISATION THAN ITS WONDERFUL ROADS. THEY ARRIVE, STRAIGHT AND RELIABLE, FROM EVERY CORNER OF THE KNOWN WORLD, AND THEY ALL LEAD TO ROME ...

LVPVS GARVM
THE ORIGINAL

ROMA →
ROMA ←
VII

CLANG

WHAT CAN I SAY! ALL IN SUCH A HURRY TO GET TO ROME, RUSH, RUSH, RUSH AND THEY DON'T SEE THE POTHOLES!

NERVUS BREAKDOWN RECOVERY

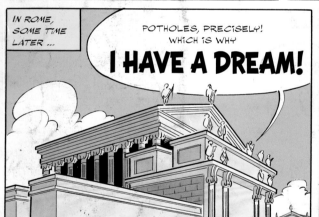

IN ROME, SOME TIME LATER ...

POTHOLES, PRECISELY! WHICH IS WHY

I HAVE A DREAM!

I HAVE A DREAM THAT PUBLIC FUNDS SHALL GO TOWARDS MAINTAINING OUR ROMAN ROADS AND NOT INTO FUNDING SENATOR LACTUS BIFIDUS'S ORGIES.

SPQR

PSSST, BIFIDUS!. WAKE UP, THIS IS ABOUT YOU!

2

OBELIX, I'LL STAY WITH GERIATRIX, YOU CAN GO FOR A WANDER WITH DOGMATIX ...

ALRIGHTIE.

GNiii

CHOP, CHOP! I'VE STILL GOT TWO GOTHS TO NUMB UP.

CAESAR THE WAR WITH THE GAULS

PERSONALISED SHIELDS

IX XCIX SESTE FOR ONLY DCLXXXI

THE END OF TRADITIONAL MENHIRS!

NOT ONLY DECORATIVE BUT LIGHTER, YOUR FRIENDS WILL BE AMAZED!

PSS!

INSIST ON GENUINE VESUVIAN PUMICE!

TOCK TOCK

WANT A NEW CHARIOT?

?

TURBOCATALITIX
NEW AND SECOND-HAND CHARIOTS

NOT ME, BUT APPARENTLY IT'S WRITTEN HERE!

?

SUPAFENDA WILL SHOW YOU OUR DESIGNS.

FOLLOW YOUR INSTINCTS. I'M SURE WE HAVE JUST THE CHARIOT FOR YOU!

WE'VE GOT ALL SORTS, GREEK ONES, ROMAN ONES, AND ALL SIZES, THERE'S THE MAXI, THE MINI, THE MICRA ...

WE ALSO HAVE THIS MAGNIFICENT GAULISH WINGED SPORTS CHARIOT!

A LITTLE LATER ...

YOU SEE, GERIATRIX, IT WASN'T ALL THAT BAD!

BY BELENOFF! I FEEL LIKE A FIKFTEEN-YEAR-OLD!

AND PLUFF I'LL GET A NEW ONE. IT WAV A MILK TOOF ... UNLEFF HE WAV LYING THROUGH HIS TEEF.

AH! THERE'S OBELIX.

I FOLLOWED MY INSTINCTS.

?!

WHAT'S THAT CHARIOT FOR, OBELIX?

WHAT? THERE'S MORE TO LIFE THAN MENHIRS ...

WELL DONE, OBELIKF! YOU HAVE TO DO VEVE FINGS WHEN YOU'RE YOUNG!

HOW DID YOU PAY FOR IT?

THE SALESMAN SAID I COULD PAY ON CREDIT. TEN INSTALMENTS OF EIGHT MENHIRS: A BARGAIN!

OBELIX, YOU DO REALISE THAT SORT OF CHARIOT IS MEANT FOR RACING AND ...

GET YOUR "CONDATUM ECHO"!

ALL THE DETAILS OF THE GREAT TRANSITALIC RACE!

7

A CHARIOT RACE ON ROMAN SOIL? HEHE! WHY NOT?

TRANSITALIC RACE

IT MIGHT BE FUN BOTHERING THEM ON THEIR HOME TURF FOR ONCE!

YOU CAN'T BECOME AN AURIGA OVERNIGHT, OBELIX! YOU WERE A MENHIR DELIVERYMAN LAST TIME I LOOKED!

PAH! TRADITIONAL MENHIRS ARE HAVING A DOWNTURN BECAUSE OF PUMICE STONE COPIES.

... AND THE SIBYL AT THE MARKETPLACE SAID ...

TUT TUT! YOU MUSTN'T BELIEVE PREDICTIONS, OBELIX. REMEMBER THE HOROSCOPE*

* SEE THE MISSING SCROLL

YES BUT THIS TIME IT'S WRITTEN ON MY HAND! SHE DIDN'T PALM ME OFF WITH ANY OLD NONSENSE!

AND WHY CAN'T I BE AN AURIGA, ANYWAY? WHY DOES ASTERIX ALWAYS GET TO BE THE STAR?

OBELIX, MY FRIEND, YOU'RE IN MENHIRS!

OH REALLY? WELL, WHAT IF I WANT TO DROP THEM?

COME ON, CALM DOWN! THE "CONDATUM ECHO" SAYS THE RACE IS FOR TEAMS OF TWO!

DEADLOCK: GERGOVIAN SOLDIERS' PENSIONS SLASHED

VETERANS OUTRAGED

PRICE OF WILD BOAR TIME HIGH

TEAMS OF TWO? WELL, THAT'S PERFECT: PUT IT THERE, WE CAN BOTH BE AURIGAE!

AURIGA-YOU AND AURIGA-ME!

THAT'S SORTED! NOW WE NEED TO THINK ABOUT HORSES BUT I'VE GOT AN IDEA FOR THAT!

OK, BUT I'M PAYING!

THE NEXT DAY...

CENTURION! FOUR OF OUR BEST HORSES HAVE BEEN REPLACED BY MENHIRS!

THAT'S THOSE CONFOUNDED GAULS! SET UP THE BLOCKADE!

CONSIDER IT DONE!

3A

GETAFIX HAS PREPARED HIS MAGIC POTION AND ENGRAVED YOUR ITINERARY, DEAR BOYS, I TRUST YOU'LL HONOUR OUR VILLAGE!

VAT'F ENOUGH! LET'F GO!

NO, GERIATRIX, YOU'RE NOT GOING WITH THEM!

OH, ITALY, THE SERENADING!

SHE WON'T GIVE YOU ANY TROUBLE! I'VE STRENGTHENED THE AXLES AND CHECKED THE BRAKES!

WATCH OUT FOR ANYTHING FISHY!

PFF!

OVERGROWN CHILDREN!

3B

10

WE'LL BE GOING THROUGH LUGDUNUM*, THEN ON TO MODICIA** IN ITALY, WHERE THE RACE WILL START.

ITALY'S GOING TO BE GREAT, ISN'T IT, ASTERIX? WE'LL SEE LOADS OF ROMANS!

* LYON ** MONZA

HALT! VEHICLE CHECKPOINT, BY MERCURY!

THOSE ROMANS MADE ME JUMP, BY TOUTATIS ...

... FOR A MINUTE I THOUGHT WE WERE THERE ALREADY.

A FEW DAYS LATER IN MODICIA, THE START TIME IS DRAWING NEAR AND TENSION IS MOUNTING ALREADY ...

OLIVE OIL FOR AXLES

LVPVS

SLOW DOWN POTHOLES

SENATOR BIFIDUS IS ON SITE ANSWERING QUESTIONS FROM SCRIBES WHO HAVE COME FROM EVERY DIRECTION TO COVER THE EVENT ...

A THRILLING MULTI-STAGE RACE FROM THE ALPS TO VESUVIUS, WITH A PRICELESS TROPHY FOR THE WINNER! LOOK, THESE CROWDS KNOW THEY'RE IN FOR A TREAT ...

JUST A MINUTE! **WHO'S FINANCING THIS?** THE ROMANS HAVE A RIGHT TO KNOW!

IT'S SIMPLE: WE HAVE A DEAL WITH LUPUS, THE BIG GARUM PRODUCER, THEY'RE SUPPLYING THE TROPHIES ...

IN RETURN, WE'VE ALLOWED THEM TO DISPLAY THEIR BANNERS AND HAND OUT AMPHORETTAS OF GARUM ALL ALONG THE ROUTE.

THE CONDIMENT LVPVS OF CHAMPIONS
THE ORIGINAL

GARUM!

THE CONDIMENT MADE FROM FERMENTED FISH GUTS, SO HIGHLY PRIZED BY THE ROMANS ...

JUST A MINUTE! IS IT REALLY AUTHENTIC LUPUS GARUM? THE ROMANS HAVE A RIGHT TO KNOW!

YOU CAN TASTE IT.

THE CO

RAAAAH, IT REALLY IS, IT REALLY IS! AND IT REALLY IS GOOD!

THE FIRST-AID CHARIOT IS OVER THERE ...

I SAY, MADMAX, THIS HOT WATER IS DELICIOUS, IS IT NOT?

IT CERTAINLY IS, ECOTAX! THIS GARUM MAKES EVERYTHING TASTE QUITE EXQUISITE!

THAT'S THE BRETON CHARIOT!

AND THE LUSITANIAN CHARIOT'S OVER THERE!

HOW'S IT GOING, BITOVAMESS?

THE AXLE'S SEIZED, UNDADURESS, PASS ME THE GARUM!

HERE ARE TWO VERY SPECIAL GUESTS, THE PRINCESSES NEFERSAYNEFER AND KWEENLATIFER, WHO'VE COME ALL THE WAY FROM THE DISTANT KINGDOM OF KUSH*

* A SMALL KINGDOM IN SOUTHERN EGYPT

WE MUST INTERVIEW THEM. OUR READERS HAVE A RIGHT TO KNOW!

YOUR ATTENTION PLEASE! THIS WAY ...

HERE COMES OUR FAVOURITE, STRAIGHT FROM ROME! THE CHAMPION WITH MCDLXII VICTORIES! THE ONE THEY CALL THE "MASKED AURIGA", THE GREAT **CORONAVIRUS,** AND HIS FAITHFUL BACILLUS!

OUR LIGURIANS WILL EAT YOUR ROMANS FOR BREAKFAST!

NONSENSE! OUR ETRUSCAN AURIGAE ARE THE BEST!

AHA! YOU CLEARLY DON'T KNOW ABOUT OUR CALABRIANS!

MEANWHILE ...

PHEW! WE'RE JUST IN TIME TO SIGN UP. LET'S GET BACK TO THE CHARIOT QUICKLY!

LOOK, IT'S A BIT LIKE THE MARKETPLACE ...

13

IN THE NAME OF *JULIUS CAESAR* AND WITH GENEROUS SPONSORSHIP FROM *LUPUS GARUM*, I, *BIFIDUS*, PRONOUNCE ... UM ...

LVPVS — THE CONDIMENT OF CHAMPIONS

"THE GREAT TRANSITALIC RACE OPEN."

... PRONOUNCE THE GREAT **TRANSITALIC** RACE OPEN!

CORONAVIRUS   CORONAVIRUS   CORONAVIRUS

LOOKS LIKE IT'S ALL ABOUT THAT ROMAN!

WELL, WHAT DO YOU EXPECT?

HE'S GOT A NICE SMILE.

IT'S A MASK, OBELIX!

THE WINNER WILL RECEIVE THE **TRANSITALIC CUP**, A SYMBOL OF OUR GLORIOUS, FAR-REACHING ROMAN ROADS ...

"... OR ITS EQUIVALENT IN SESTER ..."

... OR ITS EQUIVALENT IN SESTERCES!!!

HEHE! WE'RE HERE FOR THE EQUIVALENT, MY BOY!

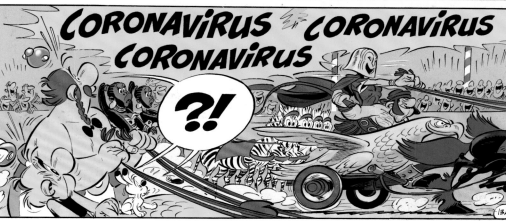

THERE HE IS! HE FELL OUT, BY TOUTATIS!

WOOF!

I'LL TUCK YOU IN HERE AND FASTEN MY BELT!

HEY, YOU FAT GAUL, YOU'RE CAUSING AN OMNI-SHAMBLES, BY ODIN!

ARE YOU COMING, OBELIX?

JUST A MO!

BÅFF

BUT ... BUT ... I WAS ONLY MAKING A STATEMENT!

ROADHOG!

Shieldhead!

AND, BY THE WAY, PUNCHES ARE AGAINST THE RULES.

REALLY?

SHOULDN'T YOU KEEP YOUR DISTANCE?

MANY ROMAN LEAGUES LATER ...

I'M NOT SURE, OBELIX. WE'D BETTER ASK THE WAY ...

PARMA? AHA! BUT IT'S BEHIND YOU!

YOU'RE IN VENETIAN TERRITORY HERE. WE LIVE ON THE WATER.

THIS IS WHERE WE'RE BUILDING VENEXIA, OUR CITY. THE GROUND'S A BIT MARSHY, BUT WHAT A VIEW! AND SO PEACEFUL!

BUT YOUR CITY'S SINKING!

NO, THE LAGOON'S RISING, ACTUALLY! THE CLIMATE ISN'T WHAT IT USED TO BE!

LET'S TURN ROUND, OBELIX!

DO ALL ITALICS LEAN LIKE THAT?

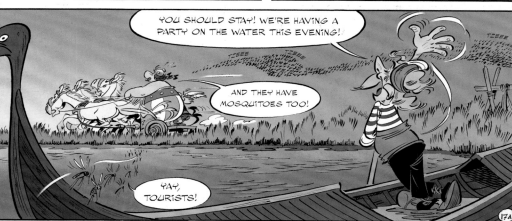

YOU SHOULD STAY! WE'RE HAVING A PARTY ON THE WATER THIS EVENING!

AND THEY HAVE MOSQUITOES TOO!

YAY, TOURISTS!

PLENTY OF COMPETITORS HAVE BEEN LESS FORTUNATE ...

OUR HOPES ARE DROWNED, MY BOY!

AT LEAST WE'RE IN OUR ELEMENT!

COME AS YOU ARE. EVERYONE WILL BE IN FANCY DRESS!

THAT WAS AN ODD DETOUR. ALMOST AS IF THE ROMANS HAD MESSED WITH THE SIGNS ...

PARMA →
OUERZO
XXI

BUT THAT'S NOT FAIR, THEY'RE VITAL!

I KNOW, WE CAN'T COPE WITHOUT THEM ...

IT COULD HAVE BEEN THE DEATH OF US!

HERE'S PARMA AT LAST!

I'M HUNGRY!

AH! OUR FRIENDS THE GAULS! THAT STAGE WAS CARNAGE! YOU SCORE I POINT!

I POINT?

THAT'S THE RULE! FOR EACH STAGE: THE FIRST TO ARRIVE GETS X POINTS, THE SECOND GETS IX, THE THIRD VIII, AND IT'S JUST I POINT FROM XTH PLACE ON!

CORONAVIRUS X
ZERØGLUT
KWEENLATI
MADMAX
WOJALOADOV

X POINTS ALREADY! WHAT GIVES YOU THAT WINNING EDGE?

A FEW WORDS ABOUT YOUR TRAINING?

WHAT'S THE SECRET TO YOUR FANTASTIC FITNESS?

THEY'RE ALL OVER THE ROMAN TEAM, POOR THINGS! THEY DON'T KNOW WHAT THE ETRUSCANS CAN DO!

YOU CAN RELAX, OUTINTHASTIX, WE'RE HERE!

IF YOU ASK ME, THAT OLIVE OIL ON THE ROAD WASN'T NATURAL!

WELL SAID, TEKAJOADOV!

AND HERE ARE THE TEAMS THAT CAME IN BEFORE YOU!

HELL OF A STAGE, BY ODIN!

AND TERRIBLE SIGNAGE!

BY ZEUS, SARMATIAN*, ARE YOU INSINUATING I SPILLED OLIVE OIL OVER THE ROAD IN FRONT OF YOU?!

* A PEOPLE FROM EASTERN EUROPE

WELL, IF YOU ASK ME COLD, IF I'M PRESSED, VERGING ON THAT, YES!!!

ALRIGHT, ALRIGHT! NO NEED FOR PRESSING, BY TOUTATIS! WE'RE ALL A BIT RUMPLED AFTER THE FIRST STAGE AND ...

?

OH MY! GUESS WHO'S SERMONISING!

ONLY THE PINT-SIZED GAUL WHO CAUSED THE OMNI-SHAMBLES!

GLUG GLUG GLUG

BAFF!

AURIGAE, DON'T FORGET: WE'RE ADVERSARIES, NOT ENEMIES! WE ALL HAVE THE SAME GOAL! PROVING TO CAESAR THAT WE CAN BEAT HIS CHAMPION!

THE PINT ... THE LITTLE GAUL'S RIGHT!

WE'RE NOT BARBARIANS!

YEAH! WE'RE GOOD SPORTS! GO ETRUSCANS!

LET'S BEAT THE ROMAN!

I SAY, IN THESE ITALIC REGIONS, ONE DOES GESTICULATE A GREAT DEAL, DOES ONE NOT?

TOCK

DID YOU SEE THAT, ZERØGLUTEN?

YES, BETAKARØTEN, THE TWO GAULS HAVE SOME SORT OF POTION.

THAT WAS WELL SAID, ASTERIX, BUT I THOUGHT PUNCHES WERE AGAINST THE RULES!

THESE SEATS OF YOURS ARE AMAZING, BY TOUTATIS!

THEY'RE BY A WONDERFUL CRAFTSMAN FROM MEDIOLANUM*, NOT FAR FROM HERE. HE HAS ALL THE LATEST DESIGNS, IF YOU'RE INTERESTED.

* MILAN

RIGHT. WHERE WERE WE? OH YES! THE HAM, OUR SPECIALITY. BEST EATEN IN VERY THIN SLI ...?!!

?!!

CHOMP CHOMP

EXSHELLENT! I'D LOVE ANOTHER SLICE.

SLURP

WHAT? SLICED HAM? THEY'LL BE HAVING POWDERED CHEESE NEXT!

A LITTLE WHILE LATER ...

I'M NOT SURE WHERE WE ARE: THERE AREN'T MANY ROMANS ...

PERFECTLY NORMAL, OBELIX. THERE'S MORE TO ITALY THAN ROMANS!

LIKE GAUL, ITALY HAS MANY DIFFERENT PEOPLES: VENETIANS, ETRUSCANS, UMBRIANS, OPICANS, MESSAPIANS, APULIANS ... AND CAESAR'S STRUGGLING TO CONTROL THEM.

20A

GET SOME SLEEP. WE SET OFF WHEN THE COCK CROWS TOMORROW.

ONE ROMAN, TWO ROMANS, THREE ROMANS ...

LATE INTO THE NIGHT, THE LAST TEAMS ARE STILL ARRIVING.

COME ON, BITOVAMESS. WE'VE REACHED THE INN.

COMING, UNDADURESS! JUST CHECKING THE LEVELS ON THE HUBS!

I POINT.

AND AT THE CRACK OF DAWN ...

♪ A-COCCALA-DOODALA-DOO ♪

BUT, UNDADURESS, WE'VE ONLY JUST ARRIVED ...

GRRR WOOF

20B

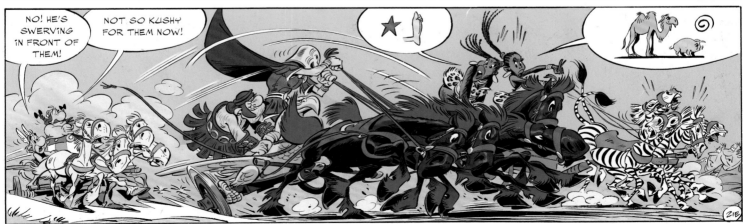

PERFECT! WHEN THEY CHANT HIS NAME, THEY'RE ACTUALLY CHANTING ROME! AND WHEN THEY CHANT ROME, THEY'RE ACTUALLY CHANTING

CAESAR!

HOW ENCHANTING, O CAESAR!

AVE, BIFIDUS! OFF YOU GO, BUT COME BACK AGAIN, CAESAR WISHES TO BE KEPT UP-TO-DATE!

I'LL HIT THE ROAD!

THIS IS FLORENTIA* WE'LL HAVE TO SLOW DOWN.

SENATE FINANCED II x II LANE ROAD COMING SOON

S P Q R

* FLORENCE

23A

GETAFIX TOLD ME ABOUT THIS NEW TOWN. PEOPLE COME FROM FAR AND WIDE TO ADMIRE ITS MODERN ARCHITECTURE AND STATUES.

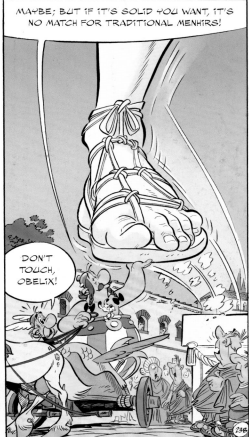

MAYBE; BUT IF IT'S SOLID YOU WANT, IT'S NO MATCH FOR TRADITIONAL MENHIRS!

DON'T TOUCH, OBELIX!

23B

AT LAST THEY COME TO SENA JULIA'S LABYRINTHINE STREETS ...

?

?

?

?

?

AND ITS FAMOUS SHELL-SHAPED PIAZZA ...

THE TOURISTS ARE HERE EARLY THIS YEAR.

CAN YOU SEE TONIGHT'S ROADSIDE INN, OBELIX?

I CAN'T SEE THE ROADSIDE INN.

WHERE IS THIS ROADSIDE INN?

IT'S REALLY VERY BADLY SIGNPOSTED!

X SESTERCES ON THE ONES IN RED!

A RACE AROUND THE PIAZZA? WHAT A GREAT IDEA*!

* ALMOST CERTAINLY WHAT STARTED SIENNA'S FAMOUS "PALIO" HORSE RACE WHICH DRAWS 20,000 VISITORS A YEAR.

THE INN'S OVER THERE BUT ONLY RESIDENTS ARE ALLOWED TO PARK THEIR CHARIOTS IN THE HISTORIC CITY CENTRE.

THAT EVENING, THE ATMOSPHERE IN THE INN IS TENSE AND THE AURIGAE ARE DEJECTED ...

ANOTHER X POINTS FOR CORONAVIRUS AND HE'S STILL IN THE LEAD! HE'S FLYING ROUND!

WHAT IF WE WEAKENED HIM WITH A BEATING?

BEATINGS ARE AGAINST THE RULES, YOU KNOW THAT!

I WANT TO GO HOME! I WANT TO GO HOME!

SUCH STRAIGHT ROADS! SUCH AN IDYLLIC CLIMATE! SUCH CIVILISATION! I CAN'T TAKE ANY MORE, SKINNIDECAF! I'M HOMESICK!

GET A GRIP, GAMEFRALAF, PEOPLE ARE WATCHING!

I PROMISE WE'LL PILLAGE AND BURN THE PLACE AFTER THE RACE ... HOW DOES BURNT SENA JULIA SOUND?

A BIT MORE COLOURFUL ... SNIFF!

HEHE! THE NØRMÅNS ÅRE GIVING UP, ZERØGLUTEN!

PERFECT, BETÅKÅRØTEN! TWØ LESS TØ WØRRY ÅBØUT!

ÅND TØMØRRØW WE CÅN HÅVE FUN WITH THØSE THÅT ÅRE LEFT!

I'M NOT SURE I LIKE THE WAY THOSE CIMBRI ARE LOOKING AT US!

RELAX, ASTERIX! YOU'RE TOO JUMPY! PROBABLY BECAUSE YOU'RE JUST A CO-AURIGA. LOOK AT ME, I'M BEHAVING LIKE A CHAMPION: I'M CALM AND ...

TWO WILD BOAR WITH GARLIC AND ROSEMARY?

HERE! HERE! HERE!

AND HERE ARE THE PASTAE, MY GAULISH FRIENDS! IT'S FROM THE EAST: THINLY SLICED DOUGH COOKED IN CREAM. EVEN IN ROME THEY DON'T MAKE IT THIS GOOD!

YOU SLICE EVERYTHING THINLY HERE!

... AND TO SEASON IT, AN AMPHORETTA OF GARUM FROM OUR SPONSOR, LUPUS.

?

WHAT EXACTLY IS THIS GARUM EVERYONE'S TALKING ABOUT?

ONLY THE **MOST FAMOUS** CONDIMENT! HAVEN'T YOU SEEN THE MOSAICS?

ON THE RIGHT BEFORE THE VESTIBULUM, PAST THE ATRIUM.

?

HERE, BACILLUS! THAT'S THE ADVANCE WE AGREED!

28A

THE SENATOR'S BANKING ON YOU TO ENSURE VICTORY FOR CORONAVIRUS.

?

THE BALANCE WILL BE PAID AT THE END OF THE RACE ... IF THE CHAMPION WINS, OF COURSE.

HE'LL WIN! I HOPE YOU REMEMBERED MY LITTLE CUT?

AND DON'T FORGET, WE ALSO SAID THE CHAMPION'S WEIGHT IN GARUM!

I'D PREFER MY OWN WEIGHT IN WILD BOAR IF THAT'S POSSIBLE ...

?

28B

AND AT THE CRACK OF DAWN, THE RACE SETS OFF FROM SENA JULIA ON TO THE NEXT STAGE ...

HURRY UP, BITOVAMESS! THEY'RE LEAVING ALREADY!

WE'RE GOING TO TIBUR* NEAR ROME IN LATIUM, VIA UMBRIA!

ERM, SAY THAT AGAIN!

* TIVOLI

MANY LEAGUES FURTHER ON ...

YOV ARE ENTERING VMBRIA
THE ROMAN ARMY IS ON A PEACE-KEEPING MISSION IN THIS REGION FOR YOUR SAFETY
SPQR

29A

HALT! ROADBLOCK!

WE'RE ON MAXIMA ALERTA! WE HAVE TO CHECK NO UMBRIAN REBELS HAVE STOWED AWAY WITH YOU!

NOW THAT YOU'VE LET YOUR OWN CHAMPION THROUGH? ARE YOU HAVING A LAUGH, ROMAN?

OOH! REAL ROMANS LIKE THE ONES IN GAUL!

!!!

WHO DARES HINDER THE GLORIOUS PROGRESS OF THE SAMARTIANS?

GLUG GLUG GLUG

NO ARGUING! RACE OR NOT, EVERYONE'S STOPPED AND CHECKED!

29B

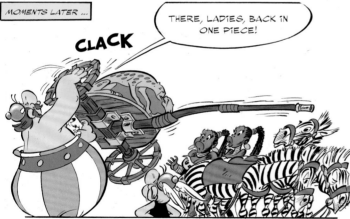

33

ON ONE OF THE MANY ROADS THAT LEAD THERE, THE RACE SETS OFF AGAIN FOR ROME, STILL PUNCTUATED BY UNEXPLAINED ACCIDENTS ...

WHEN SUDDENLY ...

THERE! THE CIMBRI!

THE GÅULS, BY ØDIN! ÅCCELERÅTE!

THEY'RE RUNNING AWAY! ADMITTING THEIR GUILT! LET'S STOP THEM!

WE'RE NØT RUNNING ÅWAY! IT'S Å RÅCE!

IT'S Å RÅCE!

CRONK

HÅVE MERCY! WE'RE JUST SENÅTØR BIFIDUS'S LØWLY SLÅVES! WE CIMBRI CÅN'T TÅKE ÅNY MØRE!

HE WØRKS US TØ THE BØNE, STÅRVES US ÅND TØRMENTS US WITH MØRSELS OF PÅSTÅE IN ÅLL DIFFERENT SHÅPES – LÅCES, RIBBØNS, TUBES, EVEN BUTTERFLIES!

IT'S TRUE, I CØ-CØNFESS! WE "LØST" SØME OF THE VITÅL ...

SP-SPILLED SØME ØIL ...

TÅ-TÅMPERED WITH Å FEW CHÅRIØTS ...

WE HÅ-HÅVE TO MÅKE SURE THE RØ-RØMÅN WINS ...

IN EXCHÅNGE, BIFIDUS PRØMISED TØ GIVE US Å SQUARE MEÅL!

BUT KEEP YOUR HÅIR ØN! IT WÅS BÅCILLUS WHØ SUGGESTED HÅVING FRESH HØRSES FØR EÅCH STÅGE ... HE ÅND BIFIDUS ÅRE IN CÅHØØTS!

AHA, SO THAT'S WHAT THE SESTERCES WERE FOR!

THE SESTERCES? WHAT SESTERCES?

AT THE ROADSIDE INN! I SAW A ROMAN HANDING OVER SESTERCES TO BACILLUS.

AND YOU TELL ME THIS NOW?!

I THOUGHT IT WAS NORMAL PRACTICE IN SPORT.

THE CIMBRI ARE GETTING AWAY!

A CIMBRI MARCHES ON HIS STOMACH, OBELIX, THEY WON'T GET FAR!

FRESH HORSES FOR EACH STAGE! EASY TO WIN LIKE THAT! THIS IS GOING TO KICK OFF NOW!

LOOK AT THIS TRAFFIC!

YES, WE'RE GETTING NEAR ROME, IT MUST BE CIVIL SERVANTS HEADING HOME.

ROMA NEAPOLIS

IMPERIAL TIBVR WELL

LVPVS GARVM

HERE'S TONIGHT'S INN. LET'S GO AND HAVE A WORD WITH OUR MASKED CHAMPION!

SWISH ROUND HERE, ISN'T IT!

LVPVS

CORONAVIRUS, THE CHAMPION? WHO WON THIS STAGE BY LEAGUES? ... HE'S NOT HERE!

HE'S A GUEST OF SENATOR BIFIDUS, WHO HAS A SMALL HOLIDAY VILLA NOT FAR FROM HERE!

MY FRIENDS, THIS GLORIOUS RACE HAS MADE ME PERSONA GRATA AT THE SENATE. THANKS TO YOU, I'M BACK TO RUNNING THE SESTERCES FOR THE ROMAN ROADS AS I SEE FIT!

AND DE FACTO TO FUNDING YOUR OWN LIFESTYLE!

LACTUS, THE ORGY'S READY!

JUST COMING, MOZZARELLA!

HEY, YOU TWO! YOU CAN'T PARK OUTSIDE THE SENATOR'S VILLA!

?!

BIFF

BAFF

LACTUS, DID YOU INVITE ANY GAULS TO THE ORGY?

BAFF

WAIT, I'LL BE BACK! WE WOULDN'T WANT THEM TO HAVE A WASTED JOURNEY.

BAFF

OBELIX! THE SENATOR!

HE'S GETTING AWAY!

LACTUS! WHERE ARE YOU GOING? THE ORGY WILL GO COLD!

WHO CARES! WE'VE GOT THE MASK! **SO, ABOUT THESE FRESH HORSES FOR EACH STAGE?**

FRESH HORSES? OH, THE DISHONOUR! I KNEW IT!

I THOUGHT IT WAS ALL TOO EASY! BUT HOW COULD I BE SURE? I JUST DRIVE, YOU KNOW. BACILLUS MAKES THE DECISIONS!

?!

HE'S PLANNED IT ALL, FROM THE START. THE MASK WAS HIS IDEA! HE TURNED ME INTO THIS ROMAN CHAMPION IDOLIZED BY THE MASSES, AND I WAS WEAK, I WENT ALONG WITH IT!

BUT HIS SCHEMING'S GONE TOO FAR! I'M GIVING UP THE RACE! I'M GOING BACK TO MY REAL NAME, TESTUS TERONE, AND HEADING HOME TO SICILY, WHERE PEOPLE ARE OPEN AND HONEST!

?!

YOU CAN'T DO THAT! WHAT ABOUT YOUR BEAUTIFUL VILLA IN CAPRI!

KEEP IT! THERE'S MORE TO ME THAN CAPRI, NO MAN IS A HOLIDAY ISLAND!

YOU EVEN SOLD MY IMAGE TO LUPUS! "AURI SACRA FAMES"٭, THE SHAME!

LET'S LEAVE THEM TO IT, OBELIX, AND TELL THE OTHERS THE GOOD NEWS!

SO YOU'RE DEFINITELY NOT STAYING FOR THE ORGY, THEN?

QUOD? YOU'RE NOTHING WITHOUT ME, YOU WRETCH!

٭ ACCURSED HUNGER FOR GOLD

MEANWHILE, AT THE ROADSIDE INN IN TIBUR, THE REMAINING CONTESTANTS ARE CELEBRATING THE MASKED CHAMPION'S WITHDRAWAL ...

WELL DONE, YOU GAULS! WE SHOULD HAVE KNOWN CORONAVIRUS WAS JUST A JACKEY FOR ROMAN IMPERIALISM!

THESE ARE PINSAE FROM NEAPOLIS. DURUM WHEAT FLATBREADS TO GO WITH THE VARIOUS PASTAE.

SO ARE ZEBRAS FODDER-EFFICIENT?

SORRY TO BE A BORE ... YOU DON'T HAVE ANY BOAR DO YOU?

LEADER BOARD
LVPVS ⚡ GARVM

CORONAVIRUS BACILLUS	XXX
NEFERSAYNEFER KVROLATIFER	XIX
OBELIX	XVIII
WOTALOADOFKOBADOV	XVII
ATTALOS	XVI
BITOVAMADURESS	VII

AURIGAE! LET'S CONTINUE THE RACE ON FAIR TERMS! MAY THE BEST TEAM WIN!

IF YOU ASK ME, THESE FLATBREADS WOULD BE BEST TEAMED WITH SOME TOPPING*!

* A REMARKABLE PREMONITION FROM OBELIX, GIVEN THAT TOMATOES ARE NOT INTRODUCED INTO EUROPE FOR ANOTHER XVII CENTURIES.

AND AS THE COCK CROWS THE CONTESTANTS RACE CHEERFULLY ALONG THE APPIAN WAY, HEADING FOR CAMPANIA, SOUTH OF ROME ...

THE INNKEEPER GAVE US SOME FLATBREADS FOR THE ROAD!

HMPH, NOTHING TO MAKE A MEAL OF!

PUTITTACROS FOR THE SPARTAN STANDARD: IS IT TRUE THAT THE RACE WAS FIXED?

VIVAJUVENTUS FROM THE LIGURIA BUGLE: ARE THEY SAYING A SENATOR'S INVOLVED?

JUSTATIC OF THE GOTH HERALD: CAN YOU GIVE US NAMES?

LOOK! THEY'RE THE ONES WHO BROUGHT DOWN THE CHAMPION!

I KNOW THEM, THEY'RE GAULS! THE FAT ONE'S CALLED OBELIX!

OBELIX! OBELIX!

HE SMILED AT ME! HE SMILED AT ME!

SO, COMRADES, DAWDLING ARE WE?

DAWDLING?

I'LL SHOW YOU DAWDLING! I'LL SHOW YOU DAWDLING!

?!!

?

?

BACK AT CRUISING SPEED, THE GAULS HAVE MANAGED TO SECURE A COMFORTABLE LEAD AND AFTER ABOUT A HUNDRED LEAGUES ...

THE BAY OF NEAPOLIS* AT LAST! AND BEYOND IT, MOUNT VESUVIUS AND THE FINISH LINE.

* NAPLES

40

LET ME INTRODUCE MYSELF: CROESUS LUPUS, THE GREAT GARUM PRODUCER!

WELCOME TO MY ESTATES. IT'S RIGHT HERE IN NEAPOLIS THAT I PRODUCE THIS NECTAR.

YOU GAULS ARE FULL OF POTENTIAL, I LIKE YOU! LUPUS ARE GOING TO MAKE YOU AN OFFER YOU CAN'T REFUSE!

A LITTLE WHILE LATER ...

GIVING US A NEW WHEEL WAS NICE BUT I DIDN'T MUCH LIKE THE CONDITION!

REALLY?

THE RIGHT TO PUT MY FACE ON HIS MOSAICS? WHERE'S THE HARM IN THAT? IT'S MODERN!

I ONLY LIKE CLASSICAL MOSAICS.

AND AFTER A HARD-FOUGHT RACE ON THE SLOPES OF VESUVIUS ...

IT'S HOPELESS! THE ROMAN'S STILL IN FRONT!

CORONAVIRUS IS BACK!

CORONAVIRUS! CORONAVIRUS!

I MIGHT HAVE GUESSED! IT WAS A TACTICAL WITHDRAWAL!

BRRRRR

HEY, THE EARTH'S SHAKING ...

THE GOD VULCAN IS WAKING ...

AND I THINK HE SLEPT VERY BADLY.

DID YOU FEEL THAT, OBELIX?

YES, MAYBE SOMEONE POTHOLING?

BRRRR

IT'S HAPPENING AGAIN!

SHE'S GONNA BLOW ...

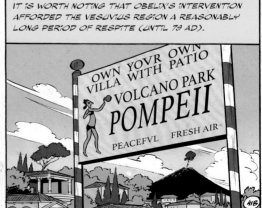

It is worth noting that Obelix's intervention afforded the Vesuvius region a reasonably long period of respite (until 79 AD).

THE FINISH LINE! I'VE GOT 'EM!

?!

CRONK

POTHOLE! POTHOLE!

OBELIX, MY FRIEND, YOU'RE ACTUALLY WINNING!

WELL? ISN'T THAT WHAT'S MEANT TO HAPPEN?

AAAAARGH!!! BIFIDUS! BIFIDUS!

THE GAULS! THE GAULS!

THEY WON!

THREE CHEERS FOR OBELIX, HIP HIP ...

HEY, LOOK AT CORONAVIRUS! HE'S TAKING OFF HIS MASK!

BUT ... IT'S NOT CORONAVIRUS!

IT'S ... IT'S ...

CAESAR, YES IT IS CAESAR! WHO ELSE COULD SAVE ROME'S HONOUR?

TRANSITALIC I

BUT HE HAS TO ADMIT HE RATHER ENJOYED THIS LITTLE RACE: ASPECTS OF IT REMINDED HIM OF HIS MISSPENT YOUTH ...

EVER THE SPORTSMAN, CAESAR RALLIES TO THE CRY OF HIS PEOPLE! IN THE NAME OF ROME AND ALL ITALY, CAESAR GIVES THE TRANSITALIC CUP TO THE GAULS!

LONG LIVE CAESAR!

HURRAY FOR OUR GREAT LEADER!

HERE'S TO ROME!

HERE'S TO ITALY!

UM ... I'VE BEEN THINKING, CHARIOT RACING'S NOT REALLY MY THING, HERE ONE DAY, THERE THE NEXT, NO PEACE, THE CONSTANT SPEED, GRABBING MEALS ON THE HOOF ...

AND ANYWAY, WITHOUT MY CO-AURIGA ... NO, I'D NEVER HAVE WON. HERE, ASTERIX, THIS IS FOR YOU!

THANK YOU, MY KIND FRIEND OBELIX, IT WAS A GREAT RACE!

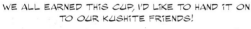

WE ALL EARNED THIS CUP, I'D LIKE TO HAND IT ON TO OUR KUSHITE FRIENDS!

NO REASON WE SHOULDN'T SHARE TOO, BY MARX!

I DISAGREE! THE CUP SHOULD GO TO THE MOST PERSISTENT TEAM: THE LUSITANIANS, BY ZEUS!

TAKE THE EQUIVALENT IN SESTERCES, UNDADURESS! WE'RE GOING TO NEED A NEW CHARIOT!

BLONK TUNK

DELICIOUS DOWN TO THE LAST DROP LVPVS GARVM

With heartfelt thanks to Anthea Bell for her wonderful translation work on ASTERIX over the years.
Les Éditions Albert René and Orion Children's Books

Asterix titles available now

ORION CHILDREN'S BOOKS

First published in Great Britain in 2017 by Hodder and Stoughton
This paperback edition published in 2018 by Hodder and Stoughton

1 3 5 7 9 10 8 6 4 2

ASTERIX®-OBELIX®-DOGMATIX®
Original edition © 2017 Les Éditions Albert René
English translation © 2017 Les Éditions Albert René
Original title: *Astérix et la Transitalique*
Exclusive licensee: Hachette Children's Group
Translator: Adriana Hunter
Typography: Arvind Shah

The right of Jean-Yves Ferri to be identified as the author of this work and
the right of Didier Conrad to be identified as the illustrator of this work have been
asserted by them in accordance with the Copyright, Designs and Patents Act 1988.

A CIP catalogue record for this book is available from the British Library.

ISBN 978-1-5101-0401-3 (cased)
ISBN 978-1-5101-0403-7 (Indian paperback)
ISBN 978-1-5101-0500-3 (paperback)
ISBN 978-1-5101-0402-0 (ebook)

Printed in China
The paper and board used in this book are from well-managed forests and other responsible sources.

FSC
MIX
Paper from
responsible sources
FSC® C104740
www.fsc.org

Orion Children's Books
An imprint of Hachette Children's Group, part of Hodder & Stoughton
Carmelite House, 50 Victoria Embankment
London EC4Y 0DZ
An Hachette UK Company

www.hachette.co.uk
www.asterix.com
www.hachettechildrens.co.uk
Asterix and Obelix

Asterix ®

Have you read them all?

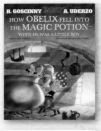